Firefighters' Folklore

North American Folklore

Children's Folklore
Christmas and Santa Claus Folklore
Contemporary Folklore
Ethnic Folklore
Family Folklore
Firefighters' Folklore
Folk Arts and Crafts
Folk Customs
Folk Dance
Folk Fashion
Folk Festivals
Folk Games
Folk Medicine
Folk Music
Folk Proverbs and Riddles
Folk Religion
Folk Songs
Folk Speech
Folk Tales and Legends
Food Folklore
Regional Folklore

North American Folklore

Firefighters' Folklore

BY ELLYN SANNA

Mason Crest Publishers

Mason Crest Publishers Inc.
370 Reed Road
Broomall, Pennsylvania 19008
(866) MCP-BOOK (toll free)
www.masoncrest.com

First printing
1 2 3 4 5 6 7 8 9 10
Library of Congress Cataloging-in-Publication Data on file at the Library of Congress.
ISBN 1-59084-334-7
        1-59084-328-2 (series)

Design by Lori Holland.
Composition by Bytheway Publishing Services, Binghamton, New York.
Cover design by Joe Gilmore.
Printed and bound in the Hashemite Kingdom of Jordan.

Picture credits:
Corbis: p. 63
Corel: pp. 16, 30, 33, 46, 58, 62, 64, 86, 88, 93, 94, 95, 98, 99, 100
J. Rowe: pp. 8, 27, 68, 82
Keith Rosco: p. 90
PhotoDisc: pp. 6, 14, 20, 28, 32, 34, 36, 38, 48, 56, 66, 78, 80
Cover: "To the Rescue!" by Norman Rockwell © 1939 SEPS: Licensed by Curtis
        Publishing, Indianapolis, IN. www.curtispublishing.com

Printed by permission of the Norman Rockwell Family
© the Norman Rockwell Family Entities

Contents

Folklore grows from long-ago
seeds. Just as an acorn sends
down roots even as it shoots up
leaves across the sky, folklore is
rooted deeply in the past and
yet still lives and grows today.
It spreads through our modern
world with branches as wide
and sturdy as any oak's;
it grounds us in yesterday even
as it helps us make sense of
both the present and the future.

Introduction

by Dr. Alan Jabbour

W HAT DO A TALE, a joke, a fiddle tune, a quilt, a jig, a game of jacks, a saint's day procession, a snake fence, and a Halloween costume have in common? Not much, at first glance, but all these forms of human creativity are part of a zone of our cultural life and experience that we sometimes call "folklore."

The word "folklore" means the cultural traditions that are learned and passed along by ordinary people as part of the fabric of their lives and culture. Folklore may be passed along in verbal form, like the urban legend that we hear about from friends who assure us that it really happened to a friend of their cousin. Or it may be tunes or dance steps we pick up on the block, or ways of shaping things to use or admire out of materials readily available to us, like that quilt our aunt made. Often we acquire folklore without even fully realizing where or how we learned it.

Though we might imagine that the word "folklore" refers to cultural traditions from far away or long ago, we actually use and enjoy folklore as part of our own daily lives. It is often ordinary, yet we often remember and prize it because it seems somehow very special. Folklore is culture we share with others in our communities, and we build our identities through the sharing. Our first shared identity is family identity, and family folklore such as shared meals or prayers or songs helps us develop a sense of belonging. But as we grow older we learn to belong to other groups as well. Our identities may be ethnic, religious, occupational, or regional—or all of these, since no one has only one cultural identity. But in every case, the identity is anchored and strengthened by a variety of cultural traditions in which we participate and

3

share with our neighbors. We feel the threads of connection with people we know, but the threads extend far beyond our own immediate communities. In a real sense, they connect us in one way or another to the world.

Folklore possesses features by which we distinguish ourselves from each other. A certain dance step may be African American, or a certain story urban, or a certain hymn Protestant, or a certain food preparation Cajun. Folklore can distinguish us, but at the same time it is one of the best ways we introduce ourselves to each other. We learn about new ethnic groups on the North American landscape by sampling their cuisine, and we enthusiastically adopt musical ideas from other communities. Stories, songs, and visual designs move from group to group, enriching all people in the process. Folklore thus is both a sign of identity, experienced as a special marker of our special groups, and at the same time a cultural coin that is well spent by sharing with others beyond our group boundaries.

Folklore is usually learned informally. Somebody, somewhere, taught us that jump rope rhyme we know, but we may have trouble remembering just where we got it, and it probably wasn't in a book that was assigned as homework. Our world has a domain of formal knowledge, but folklore is a domain of knowledge and culture that is learned by sharing and imitation rather than formal instruction. We can study it formally—that's what we are doing now!—but its natural arena is in the informal, person-to-person fabric of our lives.

Not all culture is folklore. Classical music, art sculpture, or great novels are forms of high art that may contain folklore but are not themselves folklore. Popular music or art may be built on folklore themes and traditions, but it addresses a much wider and more diverse audience than folk music or folk art. But even in the world of popular and mass culture, folklore keeps popping up around the margins. E-mail is not folklore—but an e-mail smile is. And college football is not folklore—but the wave we do at the stadium is.

This series of volumes explores the many faces of folklore throughout the North American continent. By illuminating the many aspects of folklore in our lives, we hope to help readers of the series to appreciate more fully the richness of the cultural fabric they either possess already or can easily encounter as they interact with their North American neighbors.

ONE

The Power of Life and Death
Fire in Myth and Legend

Ancient legends from many cultures explain how humans came to possess the gift of fire. According to Native American legend, Coyote gave the gift to humans, but the Greeks said it was the god Prometheus who gave humanity the fiery gift.

LONG, LONG AGO, when people were brand new, they spent much of their days in utter happiness. When the earth was warm and food was plentiful, people laughed and played. But as the autumn days grew shorter and colder, sadness fell across their hearts. They feared for their children and their grandchildren, because young bodies often died in the winter. And they knew that many of their old people, those who carried the people's sacred stories in their minds, would not survive the cold. As fall gave way to winter, the people got ready to say good-bye to one another.

Coyote did not fear the winter, for he knew he would live forever. But one day as he was passing a human village, he heard the faraway voices of women mourning for their babies and old ones. The sounds of their men's voice came to Coyote on the wind. "If only we could keep a piece of the sun with us through the winter," they were saying, "then we would no longer lose our loved ones to the cold."

Coyote felt sorry for the pitiful humans, and he decided to do something to help them. He knew that the three Fire Beings lived on a faraway mountaintop, selfishly guarding their fire for fear humans would discover its secret and become as powerful as the Fire Beings. Coyote decided to steal their fire and give it to the humans.

So Coyote went to his friends and asked for their help. Then he crept to the top of the Fire Beings' mountain—and he stole the fire. But the three Fire Beings rose up screeching, "A thief! A thief!"

One lunged after Coyote, but she caught only the tip of his tail, leaving it forever white. Coyote shouted and tossed the fire to Squirrel, who carried it on her back. She was scorched so badly that her tail curled (as squirrels' tails still do today), but she bravely carried the fire to Chipmunk. One of the Fire Beings clawed at Chipmunk, leaving a track of three black stripes behind, but Chipmunk threw the fire to Frog. Another Fire Being caught Frog by his tail, but he hopped away, leaving his tail behind, and flung the fire at Wood.

Wood swallowed the fire whole. The Fire Beings gathered around Wood, but they could not make him spit the fire out, no matter how hard they tried. They twisted Wood, they cut him, they stomped on him—and at last they gave up and went back to their mountaintop.

Coyote smiled to himself as he picked up Wood. He carried Wood to the human village, where he showed the humans how to rub Wood together to make fire. And from then on, people no longer feared winter as they had before. With Coyote's gift, the cold no longer killed them.

THIS story from the Native American tribes of western North America illustrates how important fire is to humans. Today we no longer gather around a fire on cold winter nights (unless we have a fireplace), but in one form or another, we still depend on fire to heat our homes, to help us shape our tools, to provide the energy we need for much of our daily lives. Fire is a gift.

Many ancient cultures considered fire to be the same as life. A Shawnee prophet told his followers: "Know that the life in your body and the fire on your hearth proceed from one source." The Delaware tribes' greatest feast honored their "grandfather"—fire.

According to Swedish folklore, fire has the power to ward off mischievous and evil supernatural creatures. Because of this, the fire must not be allowed to go out in a room where there is a child who has not yet been baptized. If the fire does go out, trolls may creep into the house and steal the baby, leaving a **changling** in place of the human child.

And the Algonquins spoke of their gods' immortality by saying that "their fire burns forever." Some tribes believed that the fires kindled by lightning were sacred, gifts from the Great Spirit. Without fire, life was dark and cold and dangerous. Fire gave life.

But fire is not always kind and life giving. It is also a destroyer. Early cultures knew this as well as we do today.

Some North American tribes told the story of an old, powerful man who ran to the place where earth and sky meet, and there set fire to the tall grass, igniting the earth itself. The entire earth burned, all except for those who were pure of heart. These people rose up with the flames, and became the "sky-eyes"—the stars, the burning sparks in the heavens. The earth, however, was left barren and charred. At last, the Water-Maiden carried her basket of water to the earth and restored it to life.

Fire had the power to destroy the world—and it still has that same power. The Christian settlers of North America equated fire with hell, with damnation and everlasting destruction. Like their long-ago ancestors who crept out of the darkness to stare at this strange, hot flickering thing called fire, in their heart of hearts, the settlers feared fire. They knew it was a monster to be fought.

FIRE CREATURES

Since the earliest civilizations, humans have seen fire as an **animate** and living force. Sometimes this force was **benign**; it brought good fortune and life. Sometimes, though, fire creatures were **malignant** and threatening monsters. According to some concepts, fire creatures were neither good nor evil—but they were definitely *alive*.

- In the Middle Ages, salamanders were the creatures thought to inhabit fire. Even the most educated people believed that salamanders were able to live in the midst of flames without any injury.
- The Huron and Iroquois people of northeastern North America believed in the Fire Dragon, who was responsible for Ataentsic, the mother of all life, being cast out of the heavens and thrown down to the earth.
- According to Norse mythology, the Fire Giants dwell in a place of great heat and flames. They will bring about the world's final destruction.
- The Firebird is a fabulous creature that appears in several Russian folktales. The Firebird brings good fortune to whoever possesses it.
- In the Celtic legends of Europe, the Fire-Drake was a fire-breathing, flying dragon. Its main task was to guard treasures.

These ancient concepts of fire may seem to have little if anything to do with modern firefighters. But the folklore of our civilization continues to live in the imaginations and subconscious

In ancient times, people believed there were four ele-ments—earth, water, air, and fire. Earth was thought to be the heaviest of the elements, while fire was the light-est. (The Greeks wondered if there might be a fifth element as well, one that was still lighter than fire; they called this fifth material "ether," the star-stuff of which heavenly bodies were made.) **Medieval** thinkers based their ideas of medicine on belief in the four elements.

thoughts of us all. Today, firefighters across North America still see fire as a living creature they battle. They call this creature the Dragon—or the Beast. It is a powerful and clever enemy, an en-emy that must always be treated with respect.

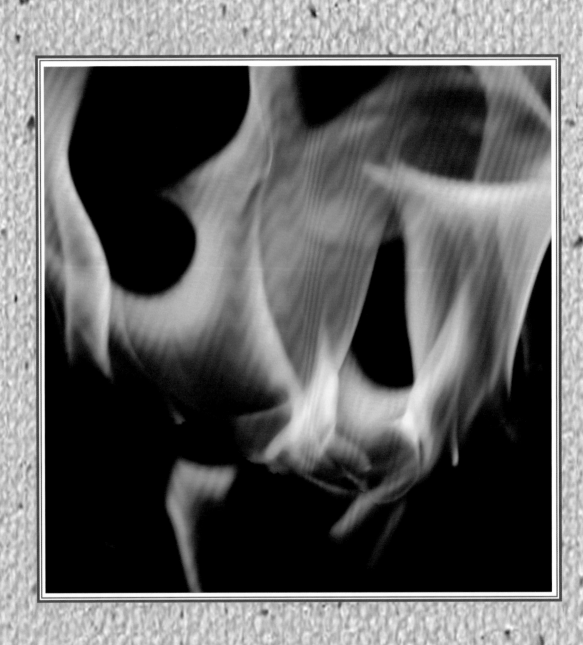

TWO

Ingenuity and Vigilance
Ancient Fire-Fighting Mechanics

Modern firefighters can thank ancient inventors for today's sophisticated hoses and pumps.

Long Ago in the second century, in the city of Alexandria in Greece, a man named Ctesibus was fascinated with the power of water. He used his study of **hydraulics** to build one of the earliest clocks, as well as a musical organ. The great genius Leonardo DaVinci built on the work of Ctesibus for many of his inventions, and today the field of robotics looks to Ctesibus as its father, for he included moving figures in his water clock.

But firefighters also have reason to thank Ctesibus for his studies. Ctesibus built the first basic hand pump that could squirt a jet of water. His invention would one day become vital to putting out fires.

In the early days of the Roman Empire, however, hydraulic pumps were long in the future. No matter how great the Romans' civilization, it was still vulnerable to fire. When an enormous fire destroyed all the wooden buildings at the center of the city, the Romans took action.

They formed a team of firefighters, called *vigiles* or "**vigilant ones**." In the event of a fire, the vigiles' job was to organize a chain of buckets filled with water to be thrown on the flames. The vigiles were also armed with ladders and long hooked poles. They used the poles to pull down burning buildings to create firebreaks.

Their organization spread throughout the Roman Empire, and the vigiles built a reputation for watchfulness and courage. Folk traditions grew up around the vigiles' exploits. These traditions continued to accumulate over the centuries, laying down a rich soil for growing the legends and folklore of today's firefighters.

But when the Roman Empire collapsed, the system for dealing with fire collapsed as well. Without the Empire to provide a backbone for the vigiles' organization, Europe was no longer prepared for fire.

At a time when heat and light were both provided by open flames, fire was a constant danger. Not surprisingly, Europe's cities were frequently devastated by fire. The city of London, for instance, suffered major fires in AD 798, 982, and 989. Fire was a dreaded and fearsome fact of life.

When the Normans invaded Britain in 1050, their strong government brought with it more organized attempts to prevent the outbreak of fire. A nightly curfew was imposed that required all home fires and candles to be extinguished by nightfall, no matter the season of the year, indicating how very serious the threat of fire was to life and livelihood. Severe penalties were imposed on anyone caught breaking the

In modern times, we continue to fear fires. Children learn about fire safety at school, and fire departments consider community education to be an important part of their job. But in today's electric world, we forget how careful earlier societies had to be of fire.

Even a hundred years ago, human beings were still deep in the throes of a passionate love-hate relationship with fire. Fire meant warmth and coziness and safety—and at the same time, it meant disaster and screaming horror. Each time someone lit a candle to light the gloom of night, each time he pressed close to a fireplace to warm winter-chilled hands, each time she leaned over an open fire to cook her family's meat, these people also risked the dangers of fire. Even a tiny candle flame could turn into a fire big enough to destroy a city.

curfew. Despite these efforts, though, in 1086 a huge fire gutted London, killing 3,000 people. And there was worse yet to come.

But in the meantime, England's attention turned to a land far-away. The Crusades, Christianity's attempts to take the Holy Land from its Muslim owners, lit the imagination of people all across Europe.

Fire fighting had its own role to play in this struggle.

THREE

The Knights of
the Crusades

A Heritage of Courage

Firefighters' heritage stretches all the way back to the brave knights of the Middle Ages.

IN THE ELEVENTH century, the Christian world was focused on a single cause: wresting the Holy Land from its Muslim owners. The Church sponsored the Crusades, and many knights set off to battle.

One group of knights, however, at first cared more about helping the sick and poor than they did about fighting. Although most of them were wealthy merchants, they saw the conditions suffered by the poor in the Holy Land, and they wanted to do something to help. They set up hospitals and hospices in Jerusalem to care for the suffering.

These knights adopted a white or silver cross on a dark background as their insignia, and they became known as the Knights Hospitaller. Later they took the name of the Knights of St. John. Their reputation for compassion and dedication spread across Europe.

As the battle between Muslims and Christians raged, the Knights of St. John were persuaded to help the knights of the crusade in their efforts to win the Holy Land. Covered from head to toe in armor, even their faces hidden, the knights were often unable to recognize friend from foe. They needed some emblem to identify them.

The Knights of St. John now took the cross as their battle emblem. They believed they were fighting for a holy cause; they were convinced they were on God's side in this war. As a result, they felt that the cross of **Calvary** was the most appropriate symbol to wear into battle.

Together the Knights of St. John and the other knights of the

Because of the knights' heavy armor, medieval battle was confusing; knights needed a sign or standard to identify themselves to each other.

Crusades attacked Jerusalem's city walls. The people inside, however, were unwilling to turn over the home that had been theirs for centuries. They fought back fiercely.

The Saracens—the Muslim warriors—threw glass bombs over the city walls. Inside each glass container was a highly flammable liquid called naptha. When enough bombs fell on the attacking knights, eventually they were saturated with naptha—and then the Saracens heaved a flaming tree over the wall into the midst of the knights. Instantly, the knights were immersed in flame.

The Saracens also used a similar technique when they fought at sea. The filled their vessels of war with naptha, rosin, sulfur, and flaming oil—all highly flammable materials—and then drove their ships into the sides of the Crusaders' vessels. The wooden ships caught fire easily, and the knights found themselves trying to escape a floating hell.

Fire was the Saracens' weapon of choice—and the Knights of St. John worked together against this new and deadly enemy. Risking death themselves, they struggled to rescue their comrades from the flames. They fought valiantly to put out the fires.

In 1530, the Island of Malta was given to these knights, and their battle insignia, the eight-point cross, became known as the

The Knights of St. John had three kinds of members:

- the Knights themselves, of whom there were never more than 600; these had military duties and came from upper-class families.
- the serving brothers, who were responsible for the sick; they were often from the middle or lower classes.
- the chaplains, who conducted the order's religious services.

Members came from across Europe, and were divided into seven groups called "Tongues": Provence, Auvergne, France, Italy, England, Germany, and Spain.

The Knights of St. John was first founded as a charitable brotherhood by a group of Italian merchants. When they were forced out of Jerusalem, they spent 18 years in Cyprus before moving to Rhodes. They ruled the island for 213 years; under their command, houses, churches, and fortifications were built.

In 1522, Suleiman the Magnificent, a Muslim ruler, laid siege to Rhodes and forced the Knights to leave.

Maltese Cross. This cross, which had originally helped the knights recognize their friends in battle, now became a symbol of heroism and service. It was considered sacred, and it stood for the principles of charity, loyalty, chivalry, gallantry, generosity to friend and foe, protection of the weak, and dexterity in service.

Today, firefighters have claimed the Maltese Cross as their own insignia. They look to those long-ago Knights of St. John as their forerunners, the earliest firefighters to join together for the purpose of saving lives from fire. Modern firefighters wear the Maltese Cross to symbolize their willingness to risk their lives for others, just as the Knights did centuries ago.

This heritage of courage is part of present-

The Knights of St. John were ruled by the Grand Master, who was elected for life by members of the order. The order still exists today.

Modern firefighters' symbol evolved from the Maltese Cross, the emblem of the Knights of St. John.

day firefighters' folklore. It helps firefighters define their identity. It gives them a sense of belonging to a long line of heroic knights, knights who had enough compassion and bravery to battle the worst enemy of all—fire.

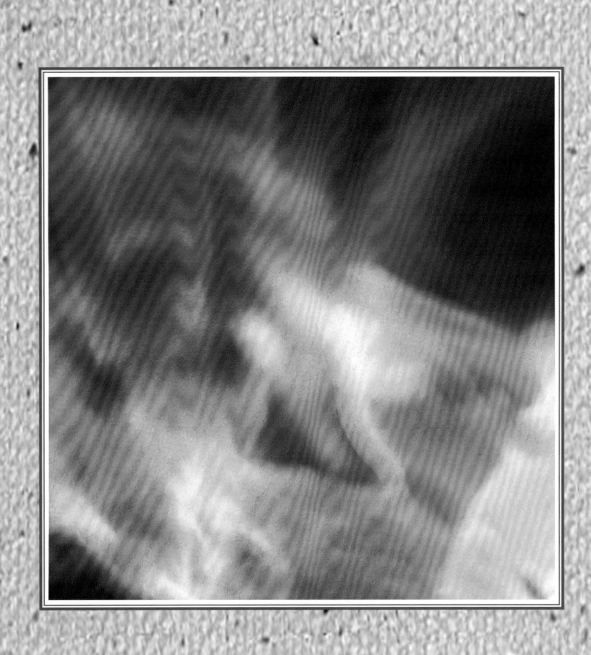

FOUR

The Flames of
Destruction
The Great Fire of London

When today's firefighters battle a blaze, they are links in a long chain of men and women who battled fire's destructive power.

BACK IN ENGLAND, the threat of fire was still so great in London that an Act of Parliament decreed that patrolmen should walk the streets at night, shouting out this reminder: "Take care of your fire and candle, be charitable to the poor, and pray for the dead."

When fires did break out, informal bucket brigades gathered around to fight it. Around 1600, the first primitive fire-fighting machines began to be used. Some people kept handheld water squirters (based on Ctesibus' ancient design) on hand as a sort of early form of the fire extinguisher. A few of London's **parishes** owned manually operated pumps mounted on tanks of water with nozzles on top. Most of these machines proved to be virtually useless for combating a big fire. Because of the open fires inside nearly every wooden and thatched building, fires continued to break out.

People may have been resigned to fire being an unavoidable danger. But in 1666, the Great Fire of London changed this attitude of complaisance.

EARLY on Sunday morning, September 2, 1666, a fire began in Pudding Lane in the house of Thomas Farynor, the King's baker. Thomas woke to find his house full of smoke and flame; he and his household (except for one maid who was too frightened to climb out the window) escaped from the house, never dreaming how great the fire would grow.

Sparks from the burning house fell on hay in the yard of the Star Inn. The inn went up in flames and spread to the nearby

Even something as innocent and lovely as candlelight can start a fire that destroys homes and lives.

Church of St. Margaret. Like a huge ocean of flame, it traveled in waves down Pudding Lane and Fish Street Hill to the warehouses and wharves along the Thames River. *Tallow*, oil, hay, timber, **hemp**, and coal were stored there along the **quays**. By eight o'clock, about six hours after the fire started in Thomas Faynor's house, the fire had traveled halfway across London Bridge. More than 300 houses were in flames.

After the Great Fire of London, fewer houses were built out of wood and thatch, and more and more homeowners built brick houses with tile roofs.

Law obligated the parishes of the city to provide their citizens with buckets, axes, ladders, squirters, and fire hooks—but most parishes neglected to maintain their equipment. Now when it was desperately needed, the fire-fighting equipment was found to be broken or rotten. The only water supply was the river—and access to the Thames was cut off in many places by the fire.

Samuel Pepys, the famous author and a citizen of London at the time, saw at once that organized action must be taken. But

Part of the problem with early fire-fighting efforts was that the firefighters could not get close enough to the blaze to battle it effectively. In the early 1700s, a Dutch engineer, Jan Van der Heiden, built flexible leather hoses 50 feet long that could be connected to each other with brass screw couplings. He used a light hand pump with these hoses, allowing fire-fighting teams to finally deliver water from a distance away to the core of the fire.

the Lord Mayor was reluctant to do anything. When asked if houses could be pulled down to make firebreaks, he answered, "Who will pay for the rebuilding?" Pepys apparently turned on his heel with an impatient sigh—and returned with a royal command that the houses were to be pulled down.

Londoners did not know how to fight the fire, though. Their firebreaks were too close to the fire and only added fuel to the roaring flames. Desperate now, they used gunpowder to blow up houses, trying to stop the hungry fire from spreading.

At last, after four days and nights, the fire finally died out. Thirteen thousand homes had been destroyed, as well as 44 **livery** halls and thousands of smaller buildings. More than 100,000 Londoners were homeless. According

Today's powerful hoses trace their history back to the 1700s.

to the records of the time, only six people lost their lives—but thousands were financially ruined. Debtors' prisons were soon overcrowded, because people no longer had the means to keep up with their financial responsibilities. The city of London would be scarred with black ruins for years to come.

During the 1600s (and for centuries afterward), people who could not pay their bills were thrown into prison until their families could come up with the needed funds. Some people languished in prison for decades.

People no longer considered fire to be an acceptable risk. Human carelessness or a stray spark could all too easily cause yet another disaster like the Great Fire of London. The cost was too great.

Insurance companies were among the first to focus on the need for better fire-fighting equipment, techniques, and fire safety measures. These companies also realized that it was in their own best interests to hire men to fight fires in the buildings they insured. They brought new fire engines to London from other parts of Europe, and they recruited watermen from the Thames River to fight fires.

The insurance companies issued to all their policyholders fire marks, metal badges fastened to the outside of buildings. This way the companies would know which buildings were insured. When a fire broke out, more than one insurance company's firefighters would often

In our world today, we take the presence of fire hydrants for granted—but back in the 17th century, firefighters were dependent on the nearest body of water for putting out a fire.

By 1721, a London button manufacturer, Richard Newsham had improved manual fire pumps with a system of air reservoirs, pistons, and levers. He mounted his pump on top of an "engine," the earliest fire engine. His largest pump could deliver 160 gallons of water per minute and throw a jet 150 feet long. The pump, however, was extremely heavy. It had to be put on a wheeled wagon and dragged by a team of men to a fire. Horses were not used to pull the fire engines until the 19th century.

turn out—but they refused to help each other and would stand by and let a building burn if it did not bear the right fire mark.

When settlers from England came to the New World, they brought with them a heritage of folklore and memories from the Great Fire of London. Their grandparents handed on stories of the fire, and it continued to live in the folk memory of North America.

Modern firefighters know how dangerous a match can be.

The colonists understood they would not survive in a hostile new environment if they did not work together. This spirit of co-operation and interdependency led them to approach fire fighting in new ways.

FIVE

A Common Enemy
The Threat of Fire in
Colonial Times

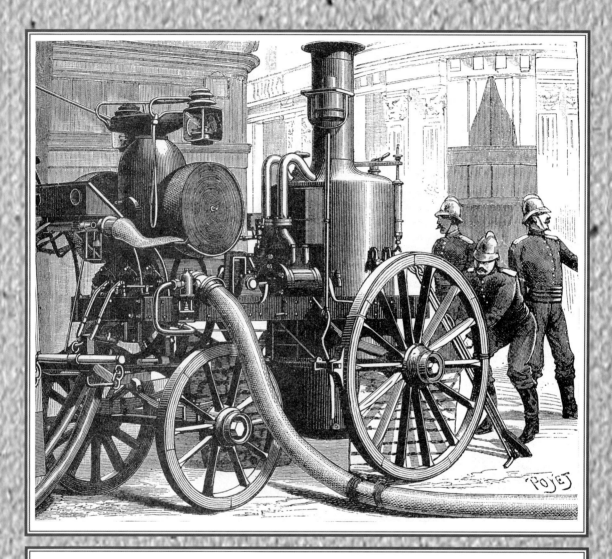

An early fire engine.

THE FOLKLORE of North American firefighters has deep roots in the Old World—but the roots are nearly as deep in the New World as well. In Jamestown, the very first English settlement in North America, fire soon took its toll on the settlers' lives.

Only a year after the colony was founded in 1607, a fire destroyed much of the colonists' food and buildings. Captain James Smith wrote these words: "I begin to think it is safer for me to dwell in the wild Indian country than in this stockade, where fools . . . burn down their houses at night."

If fire was a major danger in the small **stockade**, think how much greater that danger was as more and more people immigrated to the new colonies, forming larger settlements, all built from wood and heated by fire. The largest communities that grew up around the best harbors—Boston, New York, and Philadelphia—soon realized fire was a major problem that needed to be addressed.

In 1648, Peter Stuyvesant, the governor of New Amsterdam (which later became New York), appointed four men to act as fire wardens. These men had the responsibility for inspecting the city's chimneys and fining anyone who violated safety rules.

The city government quickly found they needed to take further measures for dealing with fire. They appointed eight prominent citizens to carry out a "Rattle Watch." These men patrolled the streets at night with large wooden rattles. If the men spotted a fire, they spun the rattles and then helped organize the sleepy citizens into bucket brigades. This was the first step America took toward organized fire fighting.

Meanwhile, in Boston, the city fathers outlawed wooden chimneys and thatched roofs. In the 1670s, however, these laws proved to not be enough to protect the citizens of Boston from **arsonists**. The city's small fire "ingine," built by a local iron-maker, could do little to fight back the wall of flames that overtook the city.

After the fire, the city sent to England for what was then the state-of-the-art fire engine. When the three-foot-long, 18-inch-wide box arrived, it held a direct-force pump that fed a small hose. A bucket brigade was still needed to keep the engine's tub filled with water.

The Boston government realized, however, that even with this brand-new equipment, they still could not depend on the haphazard efforts of citizens to battle fire. In 1678, the first fire engine company was established. Twelve men and a captain were hired to use the engine during fires and care for it between fires. The captain, Thomas Atkins, was the first fire-fighting officer in the country.

By 1732, fire engines were improved, and two new engines were ordered from Europe. Jacob Turck took charge of them. He was given a ten-pound salary and expected to

Before the days of sirens, a firefighter would alert his community by blowing on a horn.

With such narrow streams of water available to them, firefighters had little hope of actually extinguishing a fire, so saving lives and property was often their only goal. Early North American firefighters used two tools in their salvage efforts: the bed key and the salvage bag. The bed key was a small metal tool that allowed them to quickly take apart the wooden frame of a bed. (Beds were often a family's most valuable possessions.) Once the bed was disassembled, the firefighters could carry it to safety. Smaller household goods could be grabbed and placed in the salvage bags, which would then be tossed over the firefighters' shoulders and carried to safety.

keep the engines repaired out of his own pocket. At the same time, he worked on designing his own pump, perhaps the first mechanic pumper built in the New World.

Like its sister cities, Philadelphia was also contending with the danger of fire. The city was founded in 1682 by William Penn, who gave careful thought to the dangers of fire when he planned the city's location. He had seen the Great Fire of London, and he did not want his new city to ever suffer a similar disaster. River water

provided the city with a water source for fire fighting, and to re-
duce the possibility of fire, a city ordinance made chimney clean-
ing mandatory. As many city buildings as possible were built
from brick rather than wood, to further diminish the risk of fire.
By 1718, the city had purchased its first fire engine, which was
named the Shag Rag.

Penn's fire prevention efforts proved successful for several
years—until 1730 when fire destroyed much of Philadelphia's
commercial district along the river. The Shag Rag had never been
used before, and now its trickle of water proved no match for the

By the time a team of firefighters pulled the engine to the fire, they must have been already exhausted!

In the 18th century, homeowners had no fire extinguishers—so instead, they kept leather buckets by their front doors. By 1803, in Philadelphia, water from the Schuylkill River was stored in wooden trunks to be used in case of fire.

Today, the fire station has become a community landmark.

roaring blaze. In the 12 years the city had owned the fire engine, people had grown complacent. No one had thought to keep their engine maintained. Clearly, Philadelphia needed to take further steps in the battle against fire.

As the Boston, New York, and Philadelphia citizens worked together to fight fires, they began to create their own collection of stories, speech, and behaviors. Over the years, these became the folklore that is still part of modern-day firefighters' culture.

According to fire-fighting legend, the most important figure in fire-fighting history came from Philadelphia. The name of this American statesman would take its place in firefighters' folklore.

SIX

The Father of Volunteer
Fire Departments
Benjamin Franklin's Good Idea

According to firefighter folklore, Benjamin Franklin founded the first volunteer fire department.

BENJAMIN FRANKLIN—the man who invented bifocals, studied electricity, and helped draft the Declaration of Independence—is also credited with being the founder of the first volunteer fire department. His presence in firefighters' folklore still lends a certain dignified air of patriotism and American ingenuity to 21st-century volunteer fire departments.

Actually, however, Ben Franklin was not the first North American to organize volunteer firefighters. Back in Boston, some 25 years earlier, a group of concerned citizens had banded together to form the Mutual Fire Societies. Each society had about 20 members, and whenever fire struck a member of the club, all the other members rushed to help battle the flames.

As a child, Franklin had witnessed a Boston fire that devastated the city in 1711. When he lived in Philadelphia as an adult, Franklin used his newspaper, the *Pennsylvania Gazette,* to warn his fellow citizens of the dangers of fire; he also wrote often about the need for organized fire protection. He wanted to start something in Philadelphia like the "Fire Clubs" in Boston—but Franklin wanted to go one step further.

Boston's Fire Clubs protected only their own members; in the City of Brotherly Love (which is what the word "Philadelphia" means), Franklin wanted organizations that would battle a common enemy—fire—regardless of whose property was burning.

Fire blazed through Philadelphia in 1736, and Franklin knew it was time to do more than write; now he took action. He organized the Union Fire Company; Isaac Paschall was the first American volunteer firefighter, and 29 other men soon joined him.

Other famous volunteer firefighters:

    George Washington
    Thomas Jefferson
    Samuel Adams
    John Hancock
    Paul Revere
    Alexander Hamilton

Franklin's idea soon spread, and additional volunteer fire brigades were formed in Philadelphia, each having 30 to 40 men. The companies paid for their own equipment and kept it in strategic places scattered throughout town.

Poor men could not afford to join the fire brigades, however, since the members of early companies were responsible for purchasing their own equipment, as well as paying fines if they missed a meeting or a fire. As a result, the volunteers consisted mostly of wealthier merchants and tradespeople.

The early fire-fighting volunteers took names for themselves like these:

- The Fellowship,
- Hand-in-Hand Company,
- Heart-in-Hand Company, and
- Friendship Company.

George Washington

Alexander Hamilton

Thomas Jefferson

These names says something important about the way these early firefighters viewed themselves. For them, fire fighting was an act of friendship toward their entire community. It was a way for citizens to draw together and protect themselves in a spirit of

Firefighters were often seen as community heroes, just as they are today.

unity and brotherhood. Working together to fight fires was an act of both courage and love.

This spirit of heroic fellowship continues to be an important aspect of today's folk image of firefighters. Across the United States, people see firefighters as being as noble as the Knights of St. John—and at the same time as all-American as Ben Franklin.

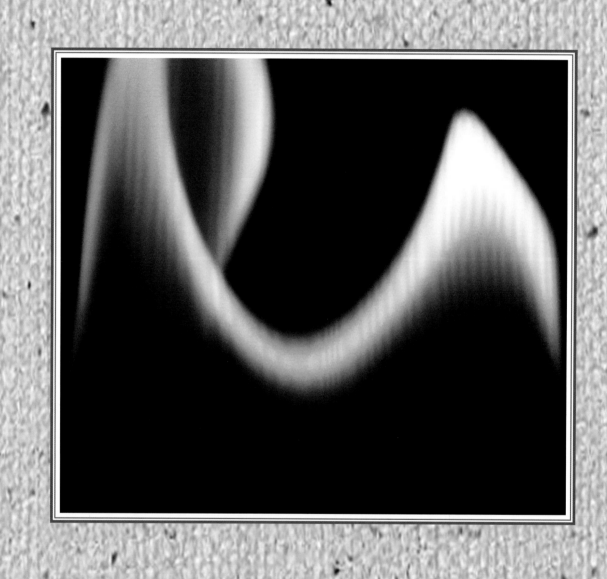

SEVEN

Willing Saviors
Voluntary Service in America

The spirit of voluntary service is still an important factor in volunteer fire companies across North America.

THE SPIRIT of voluntary service was important to the early American states. Fire-fighting historian Dennis Smith described Boston's Mutual Fire Societies as "social as well as protective associations, setting a pattern for organized volunteer fire-fighting groups, which would one day be the backbone of fire fighting in America and would dominate it for a century and a half."

In the years after the Revolutionary War, the young states took pride in their independence. Like a young adult who had just left home, they relished their sense of being "on their own"; they no longer needed to rely on mother England for protection. They could take care of themselves—and they intended to prove they were up for the job.

Militias were one expression of this sense of responsible independence. These were groups of volunteers who defended communities against the perceived (and actual) threat of attack from Native Americans and other dangers. In the early years of the new nation, militias had such a strong sense of independence that a few even stood up to the federal government, when they felt the government was threatening to tax them as unfairly as England had.

Militias consisted of both upper class and working class men, volunteers who took great pride in the fact that they were protecting their own communities. In New England, ministers preached sermons in praise of militia members, indicating that by fighting for their communities, militiamen were also fighting for God. They had a divine "calling."

As life became safer for Americans, and the threat from Native Americans less real, militias no longer had much need to fulfill

any military function. However, communities continued to take pride and enjoyment in watching their militia train. Four times a year, communities would hold "muster days," when the towns-people could gather to watch the militias perform. One observer, Sarah Kemble Knight, described her experience of these events:

. . . Youth divert themselves by shooting at the target . . . where he that hits nearest the white has some yards of red ribbon presented him, which being tied to his hatband, the two ends streaming down his back, he is led away in triumph, with great applause, as the winner of the Olympiac Games.

Militias were an important part of early America, an expression of the new patriots' sense of independence and pride, as these quotes indicate:

"I ask, sir, what is the militia? It is the whole people, except for a few public officials."
—George Mason, in *Debates in Virginia Convention on Ratification of the Constitution, 1788*

"The militia, where properly formed, are in fact the people themselves. . . ."
—"Letters from the Federal Farmer to the Republic," 1788

"Who are the militia? Are they not ourselves?"
—Tench Coxe, 1788

Militias were sources of town pride; they were a means of connecting ordinary human efforts to a sense of divine purpose; and they gave their members an identity built on brotherhood and cooperation. No wonder then that communities were reluctant to let go of them once there was no longer a need for actual physical protection.

Hostile attackers might no longer be a threat to communities—but fire continued to be. Volunteer fire companies offered former militia members another opportunity to band together in defense of their homes. These companies gave their members the same sense of dignity and importance. Building on the militias' heritage, volunteer firefighters could also claim for themselves a sense that they were doing divine work here on earth.

Before 1850, no city in North America had fully paid, full-time firefighters. Instead, across the land, people depended on bands of volunteers to protect their homes and lives from fire. During "volunteer days," fire departments from across a region would gather to compete in firemen's tournaments and participate in parades. Most of the tournaments consisted of three days of foot races, reel contests, and fire engine races. People came from all around to attend these events; in the 19th century, firefighters and their tournaments were more popular than baseball.

Today, all major cities have paid firefighters—but volunteer fire companies continue to guard smaller communities across the United States and Canada. Towns still take pride in their volunteers. These volunteers are as important to their communities as the militias once were to colonial America. People turn out to watch them in Memorial Day and Fourth of July parades, and volunteer fire companies often have annual field days, when townspeople can see firefighters' equipment and watch them

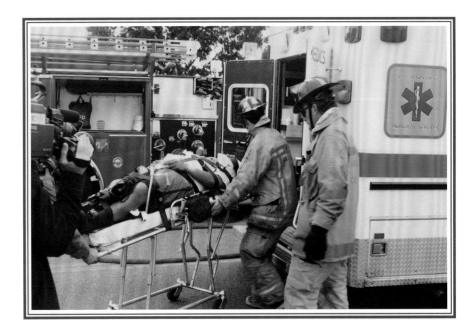

In small communities, volunteer fire departments also provide emergency medical services. They are truly the guardians of their communities, working together to keep citizens safe.

CANINE FIREFIGHTERS

A nursery school teacher was delivering a station wagon full of kids home one day when a fire truck zoomed past. Sitting in the front seat of the fire truck was a Dalmatian dog. The children began discussing the dog's duties.

"They use him to keep crowds back," said one youngster.

"No," said another, "he's just for good luck."

A third child brought the argument to a close. "They use the dogs," she said firmly, "to find the fire hydrant."

Actually, Dalmatians first worked as carriage dogs. They calmed the horses, and noblemen liked the way the spotted dogs looked running under the axel or alongside the carriage. The dogs had such stamina that they were able to run more than a hundred miles a day.

When fire engines first began to be pulled by horses in Europe, firefighters used Dalmatians to calm the horses at the fire, and to kill the rats that were often flushed out of the burning buildings. When the breed was first brought to North America in 1870, it arrived as the fire truck mascot. Today the Dalmatian is part of firefighters' folklore. Many fire companies still keep these dogs as mascots, and they often ride to fires in the passenger seat of fire engines.

Children from daycare centers and schools enjoy visiting fire stations.

perform with hose and ladder. The firefighters' hall is often used as a community center, a place for dances, dinners, and parties.

Like the early militias, volunteer fire-fighting companies are often made up of people from all classes of society. **Blue-collar** laborers and **white-collar**

professionals, people who might not otherwise interact, often enjoy serving on the same company. They are proud of their community—and they are proud to do what they can to protect that community from danger.

EIGHT

Freedom for All
Fire Fighting Beyond the
Boundaries of Race

Fire fighting was once reserved for white men only.

IN THE DARK DAYS of slavery, a rich old white man owned so many slaves he couldn't remember their names. He was kind to the smart ones and gave them the best jobs—the work that went the quickest, that didn't break backs or make fingers bleed—but the slaves he thought were stupid, he drove to exhaustion. Naturally, the people who did his work were eager to prove to him how smart they were.

One of the slaves, Little Tom, was tired of breaking his back for the old master. So Little Tom made up his mind that the master would think him the smartest of all his slaves. That night he crept inside the big house and crawled under the master's bed. Then he lay there silent as a grave, listening to the master talking to his wife.

"Somebody's setting fires," he heard the master say. "The Jenkins' barn burned down yesterday, I heard tell in town, and the Scotts' burned last week. Tomorrow night, I'm going to set a guard to watch our buildings."

The next morning bright and early, Little Tom showed up at the master's back door. "Master," he said, hoping to prove how smart he was, "I hear tell there are fires being set around about. I volunteer to guard the buildings tonight in case someone wanders around thinking to light a fire here."

The master rubbed his chin. "What's your name, boy?"

"Little Tom, sir."

"Why, Little Tom, that's a good idea. But are you sure you'd know what to do if a fire was set?"

"Yes, sir, I would."

But the old master looked doubtful. "We'll see, Little Tom, we'll see. I'm thinking the overseer would be better for the job."

The overseer was a white man, and Little Tom knew the master would never think any slave was as smart as a white man. But he decided to try to prove to the master just how smart he was. "Why don't you give me a test, sir? Then you'd know how smart I am. You could rest easy knowing I'd be able to put out any fire that might be a-burning."

So the master thought a moment, and then he pointed to the kitchen fire burning in the grate. "What's that, Little Tom?"

"What that's a fire, sir," Little Tom answered.

"No, it isn't," the old master said. "That is a flame of evaporation."

A cat walked across the hearth, and the old master said, "Little Tom, do you know what just passed by in front of the fire-place?"

"That's a cat, sir," Little Tom replied quickly.

The old master chuckled. "No, Little Tom, that's a high-ball-a-sooner."

Little Tom was getting tired of the master's games, but he bit his tongue and turned his face toward the window to hide his impatience. The old master also looked out the window and said, "Little Tom, what are you looking at out there?"

"I'm looking at a haystack," Little Tom said.

The old master laughed to himself again. "That's not a haystack, Little Tom. That's a high tower." He pointed down at Little Tom's feet. "What are those?"

Little Tom sighed. "Those are my shoes."

"No, they aren't," said the old master. "Those are your tramp-tramps."

Then the master turned and pointed through the doorway to the cook's bed in the next room. "What's that I'm pointing to, Tom?"

"A bed, sir," said Little Tom.

"No, it's not," said the master. "That's a flowery bed of ease—and you might as well stay in yours tonight, because you're just not smart enough to deal with a fire. Now get to work."

With his shoulders slumped, Little Tom went out to the field.

But that night, as he was passing by the kitchen door, he heard a howl. The cat had run through the fireplace and caught its fur on fire. As Tom watched, the cat ran out the kitchen door and made straight for the haystack that stood at the side of the yard. The hay caught fire and began to shoot flames up into the dark sky.

Little Tom knew the master had already gone to bed for the day—and Little Tom knew he'd better wake the master quick. "Master, master," he yelled, "you better get up out of your flowery bed of ease and put on your tramp-tramps because your high-ball-a-sooner has run through your flame of evaporation and set your high tower on fire."

Up in his room, the master didn't move a muscle. He just lay against his pillow and laughed. "Listen to that slave," he said to his wife, "using all those high-falootin' words, making out to be so high class."

Once more Little Tom yelled up at the window, "Master, master, you better get up out of your flowery bed of ease and put on your tramp-tramps because your high-ball-a-sooner has run through your flame of evaporation and set your high tower on fire."

The master chuckled. "That boy is smarter than I thought he was," he said to his wife.

Meanwhile, Tom yelled five more times, until his voice was hoarse. At last, though, when he saw the master wasn't going to get himself out of bed, Little Tom yelled, "Master, you better get up out of that bed and put on your shoes and come out and help me put out this haystack fire your cat started—or else your whole darn farm's going to burn up!"

"Why didn't you say so?" the master shouted as he scrambled out of bed. "If you had any brains—"

Little Tom shook his head to himself and went to get the bucket. He had plenty of brains, enough to know that if a fire's burning in a haystack, you need to put it out.

FIRE fighting was a patriotic duty and privilege. But it was one that was reserved for white men only. As this African American folktale illustrates, white men thought black men were not quite smart enough to take part in the heroic job of fire fighting. In the 1820s, in New Orleans, however, that began to change.

Earlier, in 1817, a devastating fire had swept through the city, destroying many buildings. People knew that action had to be taken to avoid such a disaster in the future. Fire Commissioners were appointed to take charge of any fire, and these men had the authority to enlist bystanders, both free and slave, to help fight a fire. By 1821, volunteer fire-fighting companies were being organized—and permission was granted to "free men of color" to organize their own fire companies.

Meanwhile, however, in Philadelphia, the city of brotherly love, white folk weren't quite so open-minded. In 1818, a group calling themselves the African Fire Association met to organ-

> Early African American firefighters called some of their company "Leather Lungs." These men seemed to be able to breath the smoke around a fire without having to come out for fresh air. Actually, these firefighters had their own secret technique: they placed their noses as close as possible to the hose streams, where they found small pockets of clean air.

ize plans for forming a fire and hose company. The white fire companies in the city responded with this resolution:

The formation of fire-engine and hose companies by persons of color will be productive of serious injury to peace and safety of citizens in time of fire, and it is earnestly recommended to the citizens of Philadelphia to give them no support, aid, or encouragement in the formation of their companies, as supported."

A committee was appointed by the fire companies to see that the African American firefighters would not have access to the city's "fire plugs" (hydrants).

The African Fire Association did not want any trouble. They abandoned their idea, and they passed a public resolution that was an apology to the community for having upset anyone.

Twenty years later, in 1838, an orphanage for African American children went up in flames. African Americans began to speak out for their rights, and public opinion about African firefighters began to change. By 1870, the city had paid black firefighters.

In Savannah, Georgia, in the 1820s, each of the city's fire companies was allowed 20 slaves. In cities across the South, slave men carried the handheld fire engine to the fires. When horse-pulled engines began to be used, slaves drove the engines. They also cleaned the stables and **stoked** the **boilers** of the steam pumpers. In Savannah, the slaves were paid 50 cents for each parade in which they marched, and they received 12.5 cents per hour while drilling or fighting fires. The first slave to arrive at the engine house when a fire alarm sounded was paid an additional dollar; the second and

In Danville, Illinois, the African American fire-fighting company played an important role in their community in the 19th and early 20th centuries. The fire station became a community center, where children from the neighborhood gathered. A pool table, horseshoes, and a trapeze were available where kids could play, and off-duty firefighters would often take the children fishing. The firefighters' stories became important to the community's folklore, as generations of children grew up hearing the same stories of heroic and amazing feats.

One of the stories that was retold again and again was the account of the fire at the Woodbury Book Store in 1915. Will Stuart and Clarence Kenner were working the fire from 54 feet up on a ladder when the wall collapsed, killing two of their comrades and breaking Stuart's arm. Kenner was thrown from the ladder and landed inside the burning walls. His fellow firefighters played the hose streams around him to keep the fire away—but what gave Kenner courage was a picture of Jesus that had fallen from the wall. Jesus' face was propped up beside Kenner throughout his entire ordeal; Kenner was convinced that it was a divine message, assuring him of his safety, and the story was repeated so many times that it became a part of the town's folklore.

third slaves received 50 cents each. The slave firemen were given badges, which entitled them to the "**immunities** and privileges of a fireman" while they were wearing them. If they failed to show up when the fire alarm sounded, their wages would be **docked**, and eventually, their badges **revoked**.

The Civil War brought tremendous change to the United States. The slaves were free—but that did not mean that white people in either the North or the South were ready to accept African Ameri-

cans as equals. The fight for equality was a long and slow one.

Volunteer fire companies enjoyed considerable prestige and political influence, and in the days of **Reconstruction**, many freed African Americans sought to achieve dignity and political power by forming their own companies. White citizens, however, often ignored and resented the black fire companies.

African Americans, however, proved to be fast, strong, and diligent firefighters. Although they were not allowed to compete with white firefighters at tournaments, white spectators began turning out to watch African American firefighters compete against each other. Respect grew for the black firefighters.

In some cities, a sense of **camaraderie** began to grow between white and black firefighters as they often worked together to put out the same fires. Their common cause put a few holes in the wall of prejudice that separated whites from blacks.

By the **Depression** years, African Americans had their own paid and volunteer fire companies across North America. Most of these were respected by both their fellow firefighters and by their fellow citizens. For blacks as for whites, belonging to a fire company was a source of dignity and pride. That pride is clear in this 1937 interview of an African American firefighter:

My daddy was a member of the old Volunteer fire company, and as I followed him in his love for fishing and hunting, I also belonged to the Volunteer fire company. . . . We were known as the "dirty dozen." There were several different companies and we had great times together, even if we were always trying to do just a little bit better than the other company. I still have a medal that was given my father by his old company for his good service in

1873. I was one of the first ones that stayed on the fire department when it organized as a paid department in 1900.

African Americans were not happy, however, that they had to have fire companies separate from white firefighters. In the 1940s, in Los Angeles, the fire chief began working toward **integration**; many African Americans, though, did not think he was moving fast enough. His reply was, "The chief engineer's responsibility is not to engage in any social experimentation." African American firefighters did not see integration as a "social experiment"; instead, they knew it was their constitutional right. Tempers flared on both sides; white firefighters began a campaign, including fund-raising, to support the fire chief in case the African Americans took the matter to the courts.

By the 1950s, the LA firefighters were technically integrated—but there were 2,500 whites on the fire department and only 74 African Americans. Meanwhile, census figures showed that blacks accounted for 10 percent of the city's population—and only 3 percent of the department's members. Black firefighters were also denied promotions above that of captain's rank.

Although today's firefighters are integrated, with blacks and whites working side-by-side, race continues to be an issue in some city fire departments. Some departments have organizations where African American firefighters can meet to discuss their problems and support one another. One of these in Columbus, Ohio, is called the African American Firefighters' Association. Their motto is: *African by Nature—American by Experience.*

THE STORY BEHIND A FIRE STATION TRADITION

On October 8, 1917, the Great Chicago Fire destroyed 18,000 buildings (about two-thirds of the property value in the entire city), and between 200 and 300 people were killed. One of the fire companies that fought the fire was Station 21, an all-black company who were often among the first on the scene at any fire.

These firefighters had a secret: they had discovered that they could quickly descend from the hayloft (which served as their bunkroom) by sliding down one of the building's support beams. Their captain noticed what they were doing, and decided to take things one step further. He sanded a wooden pole smooth and worked oil into it until its surface was slick. Then he got permission from his superiors to cut a hole in the bunkroom floor and install the pole. Now when the men heard the fire alarm, they could quickly slide down the pole and be on their way.

His experiment worked, and the wooden pole was eventually replaced with a brass one. The idea caught on and spread from fire station to fire station, until the brass pole has become a traditional fixture of all fire stations.

Eventually, the **NAACP** took the case to court. In response, 1,700 white firefighters threatened to quit or retire if blacks were assigned to their stations. **White supremacy** groups throughout the United States flooded fire stations with hate mail.

In the end, though, justice prevailed. The landmark Supreme Court decision of *Brown vs. the Board of Education* applied to school **desegregation**—but the implications for firefighters were obvious. The city commission agreed that integration was necessary.

Tensions were too high for integration to come easily. Both black and white firefighters who continued to oppose integration were transferred to what the men referred to as "hate houses." The firefighters who were forced to serve here were subjected to **hazing** and harassment. A group of black firefighters called themselves the "Stentorians" (from the Greek word *stentor*, meaning "powerful voice") and took upon themselves the responsibility of guarding their fellow African American firefighters.

Today people from different races serve together on their communities' fire departments.

Eventually, integration was achieved, both in the LA fire department and across North America. Tradition is important to firefighters, and it took time to build new traditions, ones that were based on a brotherhood that crossed the barrier of race.

NINE

A New Tradition
Fire-Fighting Sisters

Molly Williams was the first known woman firefighter.

IN 1851, the fire alarm sounded through the streets of San Francisco. Volunteers for the Knickerbocker Company No. 5 dashed to the fire station and began to lug the engine to the scene of the fire. Unfortunately, not enough men had turned out to carry the heavy fire engine.

As the men struggled through the streets, the Manhattan No. 2 and the Howard No. 3 companies passed them, shouting jeers over their shoulders at the struggling Knickerbocker volunteers. Soon bystanders began to call insults as well, teasing the Knickerbockers for their weakness and poor turnout.

Fifteen-year-old Lillie Hitchcock, however, did not join in the name-calling. Instead, she took action. She saw an empty spot on one of the ropes that pulled the engine, and she dashed into the street and grabbed the rope in her own hands. Pulling with all her strength, she shouted to the crowd that had gathered, "Come on, you men! Everybody pull and we'll beat them yet!"

Lillie was a teenager from an upper-class family, expected to spend her days socializing in pretty party dresses. But from that day on, Lillie was fascinated with fire fighting. She showed up at so many fires that the Knickerbocker Company gave her an honorary membership. She grew up and married Howard Coit, but she did not lose her interest in fire fighting.

As she grew older, she no longer followed the engines to fires. Instead, she visited injured firefighters and sent flowers whenever one died in the line of duty. Throughout her life, she wore a gold number 5 pinned to her dress, and she always signed her letters, "Lillie H. Coit, 5." When she died, her will provided funds to build a monument to honor volunteer firefighters.

 THE firefighters in San Francisco admired and respected Lillie Hitchcock's determination and spunk enough that they made her an honorary member—but they did not allow her to become a *real* member of their company, nor would they have extended the privileges they gave Lillie to females in general. In the minds of most men, women belonged in the home. Their job was to provide the family with sustenance and nurturing, while the males took on the more strenuous and adventuresome of life's tasks. Despite men's ideas, however, women went ahead and proved them wrong.

Firefighters belong to a brotherhood knit together by strong bonds of tradition and loyalty. White male firefighters were reluctant to allow blacks into their brotherhood—but they were even more reluctant to permit *sisters* into their ranks.

In today's world, however, women have fought hard to prove they are equal to men in intelligence and dedication. They have demonstrated that they have the ability, strength, and determination to do almost any job. Today's fire-fighting departments, both paid and volunteer, are all the stronger because women are allowed to join. But it has not been an easy road for women to take.

The first known woman firefighter was an African American named Molly Williams. She was held under slavery by a member of the Oceanus Engine Company No. 11 in New York City, and she showed

up to fight fire after fire wearing a calico dress and a checked apron. According to the men in her company, she was "as good a fire laddie as many of the boys." In the blizzard of 1818, when male firefighters were hard to find, Molly took her place with the men on the dragropes and pulled the pumper through the deep snow.

In the 1820s, another woman, Marina Betts, claimed a place on the bucket brigades that fought fires in Pittsburgh. A tall and dignified French-Indian woman, Marina had a quick temper and a sharp tongue. She could pass buckets as quick as any man and all the while scold any male bystanders who weren't working too. She was even known to douse an idle male with a bucket of water.

Twenty-year-old Adelheid von Buckow was another woman with the courage to step forward and do a job she saw needed doing. In 1875, she worked all night long to fight a huge blaze in Atlantic City, New Jersey. She pumped water with an old hand pumper, amazing the members of the company with her strength and endurance. Several years later, Adelheid married one of the members of the company, and eventually they voted her into membership.

Used to helping their husbands with hard farm labor, many wives of firefighters stepped in to help their husbands fight fires as well. In the early 19th century in Los Angeles, the city even encouraged the formation of all-woman fire-fighting companies. Although the male companies did not take their "sisters" seriously, the women worked hard and proved—to themselves at least—that they were strong enough for the job.

Not until World War II, however, did women's accepted role in North American society begin to change. With so many men away at the war, women had to take over men's jobs—including fire fighting. Many fire departments were turned over to women.

Today more than 5,000 women hold career fire fighting and

Across North America, women serve as firefighters, climbing ladders, handling hoses, driving trucks . . . with the same courage and dedication as their brother firefighters.

Most women do not have the upper body strength men possess, which some people believe puts them at a disadvantage for fighting fires. Jo Carol Hamilton, however, the first woman fire chief in the state of Arkansas, is only five feet and three inches tall, and she weighs only 105 pounds—and yet she says, "I can normally handle an inch-and-a-half hose by myself. Yet I've seen it knock down big men who don't know how to handle it. The difference is all in knowing how."

The Dragon Slayers, Aniak, Alaska's all-girl rescue crew, prove that women can be strong firefighters. The girls are all 15 to 19 years old (they're not allowed to enter burning buildings until they're 18), and they operate pumper trucks; drag 70-pound, 50-foot hoses; read cardiac monitors; and fly with **medevac** pilots. Being a firefighter has made a big difference to each of these girls. "Now I know I can do anything," says Mariah Brown, one of the Dragon Slayers, "especially when people think I can't. I just say, 'Watch me.'"

fire officers' positions in the United States, and they have hundreds of counterparts in Canada and around the world. They have a long and courageous tradition they celebrate each time they do battle against fire.

The courage of modern firefighters inspires us all.

TEN

Heroes for Today
Modern Firefighters

Since the events of September 11, 2001, firefighters have become the heroes of our modern world, symbols of courage and compassion in the face of evil and terror.

On THE MORNING of April 19, 1995, shortly after parents had dropped their children off at a daycare center in the Murrah Federal Building in downtown Oklahoma City, something horrible happened. A bomb inside a truck exploded, blowing half of the nine-story building into oblivion.

Americans were shocked and grief-stricken. Things like this weren't supposed to happen, not here in America where children were thought to be safe from the threat of terrorism. Saddened and stunned, the nation watched as firefighters and other rescue workers pulled the bodies of men, women, and children from the rubble. One photograph became a sort of icon for this tragic period: a picture of a firefighter holding a dead child in his arms, his grief and pain written plain on his face. That unknown man came to represent a new brand of hero, a grieving and yet strong and compassionate savior—the firefighter.

When terrorism struck America again on September 11, 2001, firefighters once more stepped in as heroes; hundreds sacrificed their lives in the burning Twin Towers. Struggling to rescue victims from the collapsing skyscrapers, they became victims themselves. Meanwhile, their fellow firefighters worked on, courageously, tirelessly, fighting to save as many people as they could. In the days after the attack, firefighters worked against the clock to find survivors in the rubble. When no survivors could be found, they kept on, searching for the bodies.

As the nation reeled, torn between shock and sorrow and anger, people desperately needed to make sense out of a world that no longer made any sense at all. In our ultra modern world, people continue to use the ancient methods of shaping reality into packages we can fit into our minds. Just as long-ago cultures turned to mythic heroes for comfort and hope when the world seemed terrifying and threatening, today we too cling to our modern-day versions, men and women who stand out against the darkness of evil because of their courage, their self-sacrificing compassion, their strength, and their commitment.

On the Halloween that followed September 11, 2001, firefighter costumes were more common than any other, indicating how quickly firefighters had taken the place of other superheroes in children's folklore.

Firefighters have become the modern-day counterparts of the ancient Greeks' Atlas and Hercules. In contemporary folklore, they are today's version of the Middle Ages' brave knights and powerful saints. Firefighters have taken their place in our unspoken folk traditions, representatives of the hero gods who loved humanity enough to give their lives.

In the days since the terrorist attacks of September 11, 2002, firefighters' brave deeds have been commemorated in songs and poems. These traditional vehicles of a culture's folklore were once sung and recited around the fire; today they are posted on the Internet. One example is "The Fire Fighter's Creed":

When I'm called to duty, God,
Wherever flames may rage,
Give me strength to save a life,
Whatever be its age.

Help me to embrace a little child
Before it is too late,
Or save an older person from
The horror of that fate.

Enable me to be alert
To hear the weakest shout
And quickly and efficiently
To put the fire out.

I want to fill my calling and
To give the best in me
To guard my neighbor and
Protect his property.

And if, according to Your will,
I have to lose my life,
Bless with your protecting hand
My children and my wife.

After terrorists attacked the World Trade center, firefighters from across North America came to help in the rescue effort.

Modern firefighters use protective equipment and gear to battle fires from hazardous material.

The same anonymous web-site author comments, "If Prometheus were worthy of the wrath of heaven for kindling the first fire upon earth, how ought all the Gods to honor the men who make it their professional business to put it out?"

Poems like these sentimentalize a firefighter's life. However, firefighters are ordinary human beings as well as heroes. These men and women have their own collection of folk traditions, and these traditions give them strength to do a physically dangerous and emotionally demanding job.

"Heroes bracelets," shiny metal bands that bear the name of a firefighter killed in the 9/11 attacks, are now being worn by teenagers and adults.

Many of these traditions grew from humanity's fire folklore and from the long legacy of stories that stretch back thousands of years. Dennis Smith, author of *Report from Engine Co. 82*, writes "In the department, you're presented with a collective memory of the many people who lost their lives in the course of duty before you. Then, as you go forward, you feel more and more that you are a part of this great tradition of brave people. That collective memory is the thing that inspires firefighters to continue, even after a great, great disaster like the one that took place on September 11th."

But not all of the folk traditions that give firefighters strength are noble and lofty; some are things as easily overlooked as ways of talking and joking.

Firefighters have their own slang. For instance, as we mentioned in chapter one, a fire is often called "the Beast" or "the Dragon." Firefighters also refer to fire as "the animal" and "the orange man." "Truckies" are the firefighters who ride the fire trucks; they have two jobs—rescue and control of the fire's direction. The person who drives the truck is called the "chauffeur." A "probie" is a

As this firefighter battles a fire, in the minds of many, he stands for the battle against evil.

new (or probational) member of the department. The hose nozzle is called the "tip," the "knob," or the "pipe." Using a unique vocabulary all their own bonds firefighters together. It helps them feel they are inside a special group, a group that forms sheltering walls around itself.

Firefighters also have a long tradition of pulling practical jokes on each other. They use humor to lighten the seriousness of their job, as this story from Dennis Smith's *Firefighters: Their Lives in Their Own Words* illustrates:

Immediately following the 9/11 attacks, then New York Mayor Rudolph Guiliani traded his suit and tie for hats and windbreakers bearing the logos of the fire and police departments. And celebrities from rock star Paul McCartney to Yankees manager Joe Torre took to wearing the FDNY (Fire Department of New York) logo.

. . . John and I went out on a medical call. On our way back from the call, we decided to pay Bill a surprise visit at Station 2. Bill, who is six foot six, was sprawled on his bed, asleep. John and I sneaked into the dorm with a bucket of cold water and dumped it on him. And I'll tell you, I thought he was going to die. I've never heard anybody scream like that.

Smith also includes this story in his book:

There was this big lug, a kind of wise-guy probie, who weighed around 220. The older guys wanted to set him straight. So Jerry "Albright says, "I'll bet I can lift you [off the ground]."

The probie says, "You can't do that. . . ." And he says, "I'll bet you. What do you want to bet?"

Jerry says, "Ten dollars."

The big probie says, "Okay, you're on." He agrees that Jerry will try to lift him up through the pole hole by means of a rope. So they lower the rope through the pole hole and attach the bowline-

on-a-bight to him, a rescue harness knot. Jerry has the other end of the rope upstairs.

Well, it took three other guys to help Jerry, and they lift this heavy probie eight feet off the floor, then they tie the rope to the safety gate. So now here is the probie hanging down the pole hole, eight feet off the ground. So of course, the guys start up the engine, put the booster line on, and completely saturate him from the booster tank. He couldn't even take some weight off himself by holding on the brass pole, because the pole was slippery from the water. So the guy says, "Okay, okay, you proved your point."

But perhaps the tradition that is most important to firefighters is the sense of family they find within the fire department. As one of the firefighters in Dennis Smith's book says, "We're a pretty close-knit group here. You've got to be in this kind of work. It's either somebody is going to cover your back or you're going to have to cover somebody else's."

Another firefighter in Smith's book mentions how good it feels to work together to help people. "I guess it's like a pitcher pitching a no-hitter. . . . everybody feels good, and they're all smiling. You're out at twenty below at four in the morning, but. . . . You get back, and you sit around and have coffee and talk about it. That feeling is great."

The firefighter goes on to say, "The only reason those guys did it was because they felt about it the same way I do. Why else would a

Firefighters may also use sarcasm and dry humor to help them cope with their work's tension. Dennis Smith tells of two firefighters climbing a smoky staircase; one comments, "Did you know this is bad for your health?"

Firefighters must be able to depend on each other completely as they enter a fire.

person do the job for the money you make? It's because you like it, and because of the tradition."

That tradition reaches back all the way to ancient people who stared in wonder, fear, and gratitude at a flickering fire. The tradition has deep roots in the stories of ingenious inventors and vigilant guards who fought fire in long-ago Greek and Roman communities, and the tradition took on new elements in the great fires that

A TRADITION OF RISK-TAKING

According to one of the firefighters in Dennis Smith's book: "We love risk taking as firefighters. That attracts a lot of us. We are a nation of risk takers, who do not believe in absolute safety. Perhaps it's in our genes from those Europeans who chose to leave the old, established life and embark on a new one at great risk."

Firefighters who take part in community education activities are also heroes.

What makes a person willing to risk his or her own life by entering an inferno like this?

swept through Europe's medieval cities. In the New World, the tradition gained a unique flavor all its own, one of independence and community spirit. As firefighters opened their ranks to African Americans and women, firefighters' folk heritage grew still richer. As recently as September 11, 2001, this tradition was growing in new ways—and so long as fire threatens humanity, firefighters' traditions of courage and dedication will continue to spread and deepen.

Further Reading

Gorrell, Gena. *The Story of Firefighting.* Toronto: Tundra Books, 1999.

Smith, Dennis. *Dennis Smith's History of Firefighting in America: 300 Years.* New York: Dial, 1998.

Smith, Dennis. *Firefighters: Their Lives in Their Own Words.* New York: Broadway Books, 2002.

Smith, Dennis. *Report From Engine Company 82.* New York: Little Brown & Company Publishers, 1999.

Riddle, John and Rae Simons. *Firefighter.* Philadelphia: Mason Crest Publishers, 2003.

For More Information

The Great Fire of London
www.jmcall.demon.co.uk/history.htm

History of Black Firefighters
www.aol.com/_ht_a/fireriters/index.html?mtbrand=AOL_US

The History of Fire Fighting
www.thefireservice.co.uk/history.htm

The History of Volunteer Fire Fighting
firefighterrealstories.com/volunteer.html

Militia History
www.resnet.wm.edu/~jmmovi/

Women in Fire Fighting
www.wfsi.org/history.html

Glossary

Animate Possessing life.

Arsonists People who set fires on purpose to cause destruction to others' property.

Benign Kindly, harmless.

Blue-collar Having to do with workers whose jobs require them to wear protective clothing.

Boilers Steam generators.

Calvary The site of Christ's crucifixion.

Camaraderie A feeling of closeness based on friendship and common experience.

Changling A supernatural child secretly exchanged for a human child.

Depression The period in American history from about 1929 to 1939, when unemployment was high and money was scarce.

Desegregation The process of ending segregation so that different races are mixed together in schools and other social settings.

Docked Fined by deducting wages.

Hazing Harassing.

Hemp A natural fiber used for making rope.

Hydraulics The scientific study of the practical applications of moving water.

Immunities Freedoms from certain negative consequences.

Integration The process of mixing races together as equals.

Livery Feeding, stabling, and caring for horses for pay.

Malignant Destructive, evil.

Medevac Having to do with the emergency transportation of sick or wounded people, usually by helicopter.

Medieval Having to do with the Middle Ages, the period of European history from about AD 500 to 1500.

NAACP The National Association for the Advancement of Colored People, an organization that acts as an advocate for African Americans.

Parishes Divisions of a city or region based on churches in the area; also a local unit of government.

Quays Structures built parallel to the bank of a waterway for use as landing places.

Reconstruction The period in American history after the Civil War, when the South was being rebuilt.

Revoked Took back.

Stoked Fed a fire.

Tallow The white fat from cattle and sheep used in soap, candles, and lu-. bricants.

Vigilant Watchful.

White-collar Having to do with the class of salaried workers who do not require protective clothing to do their jobs.

White supremacy Having to do with the belief that the white race is better than all others.

Index

Biographies

Ellyn Sanna has authored more than 50 books, including adult nonfiction, novels, young adult biographies, and gift books. She also works as a freelance editor and helps care for three children, a cat, a rabbit, a one-eyed hamster, two turtles, and a hermit crab.

Dr. Alan Jabbour is a folklorist who served as the founding director of the American Folklife Center at the Library of Congress from 1976 to 1999. Previously, he began the grant-giving program in folk arts at the National Endowment for the Arts (1974–76). A native of Jacksonville, Florida, he was trained at the University of Miami (B.A.) and Duke University (M.A., Ph.D.). A violinist from childhood on, he documented oldtime fiddling in the Upper South in the 1960s and 1970s. A specialist in instrumental folk music, he is known as a fiddler himself, an art he acquired directly from elderly fiddlers in North Carolina, Virginia, and West Virginia. He has taught folklore and folk music at UCLA and the University of Maryland and has published widely in the field.